Nick Warburton

Illustrated by Chris Molan

OXFORD
UNIVERSITY PRESS

OXFORD

UNIVERSITY PRESS

Great Clarendon Street, Oxford OX2 6DP

Oxford University Press is a department of the University of Oxford.
It furthers the University's objective of excellence in research, scholarship,
and education by publishing worldwide in

Oxford   New York

Auckland   Cape Town   Dar es Salaam   Hong Kong   Karachi
Kuala Lumpur   Madrid   Melbourne   Mexico City   Nairobi
New Delhi   Shanghai   Taipei   Toronto

With offices in

Argentina   Austria   Brazil   Chile   Czech Republic   France   Greece
Guatemala   Hungary   Italy   Japan   Poland   Portugal   Singapore
South Korea   Switzerland   Thailand   Turkey   Ukraine   Vietnam

Oxford is a registered trade mark of Oxford University Press
in the UK and in certain other countries

British Library Cataloguing in Publication Data
Data available

ISBN: 978-0-19-918462-0

5   7   9   10   8   6

Available in packs
Stage 16 More Stories A Pack of 6:
ISBN: 978-0-19-918446-0
Stage 16 More Stories A Class Pack:
ISBN: 978-0-19-918463-7
Guided Reading Cards also available:
ISBN: 978-0-19-918465-1

Cover artwork by Chris Molan

Printed by Great Britain by
Ashford Colour Press, Gosport, Hants

1

In the phone bubble

Zak looked at the picture of the rats and
shuddered.

He put the paper away in his school bag.
He couldn't put the thoughts away, though.
Or the fear. And the picture of the rats stayed
in his mind. Their teeth bared, their tails like
whips.

He was sitting on the front step of the
Foster Building waiting for Helen. Grace City
towered above him, great pale blocks
stretching so far up he couldn't see the tops.
He heard the swish of a glass door and looked
round to see Helen smiling down at him.

'Great morning,' she said. 'We should walk to school.'

'Walk?' Zak said, getting up slowly. 'It's safer by free-cab.'

'This is the safest city in the world,' she laughed. 'Come on, let's walk.'

Everyone said the friendship between them was a strange one. Zak hardly had a word to say for himself and did his best to stay in the background. He was too quiet for his own good, they said. Helen, though, fizzed with energy and talked non-stop. Those two, people said, they're like chalk and cheese.

Helen began to stride up the Avenue, leaving Zak to scoop up his bag and run after her.

'But we can't walk,' he said. 'What about the rats?'

'The rats are in the South Sector, Zak. They're not here, are they?'

'So far,' he said hurrying to keep up. 'But two more people were attacked last week. I was just reading about it in the paper . . .'

'I know. It also said the rats are being dealt with, so we're perfectly safe, aren't we?'

So they walked on, stepping in and out of sharp shadows cast on the yellow-stone sidewalk. After a while a free-cab hissed alongside and hovered, but Helen shook her head and it pulled away empty. Then another came sliding by, with a smiling face pressed to the window. Little Eddie from their school. They saw his eyebrows arch with surprise, and Zak guessed what he was thinking.

They're walking! You wouldn't catch me walking.

They paced along the Avenue until they came to a huge banner stretched across the entrance to a side-street. A familiar face smiled down from the banner. A woman's face. Big letters over it said 'BOON FOR MAYOR.'

'Hey! D'you reckon she's got her face on both sides?' Helen asked, and she stepped into the side-street to take a look.

The same face was there again, with the same smile, but the words were different. 'I'M HERE BECAUSE I CARE.' Helen turned and nodded down the side-street.

'Come on,' she said. 'This must come out on Gordon Way. A short cut.'

The side-street was deserted and Zak didn't

like the look of it. A gloomy place, hemmed in by dark-glass buildings and never touched by the sun. He looked back nervously at the bright Avenue and hesitated. He could still see the smiling face on the banner, but only just.

He thought too much, that was the trouble. He imagined things and then worried about them. Sometimes he wished he could be more like Helen, sailing through life without a care.

'But there's no one about,' he said.

'Good,' she laughed, and led them further in so that the face became lost, blocked out by buildings.

They reached an alley and stopped by one of the old-style phone bubbles on the corner. A dead-end, cold and empty. Half way down was a white van with darkened windows, and that looked empty, too.

'Come on, Helen,' said Zak. 'There's nothing down there.'

But almost at once he caught sight of a movement in the thick shadows. At first he thought it was some scrap of tumbling rubbish, but there was no breeze down there, and Grace City had no litter. The thing moved again. It was brown and grey, sliding along the base of a wall and coming out of the darkness in panicky stops and starts. When Zak saw the flick of a tail like a thin whip, and small pink feet, a chill washed through his body and his stomach lurched.

The rat stood on its hind legs, vivid and

alive, sniffing the air. Then it fixed them with
small black eyes as sharp as nails and came
scuttling straight for them. It was bigger than
a rat should have been, but that wasn't the
worst of it. There was something frenzied
about it, something unnatural.

For a second Zak stood there, frozen
with fear. Then the creature made a
dash for them. Helen grabbed him
by the wrist and pulled him
towards the phone bubble.
They tumbled in and slammed
the door. The rat reared up,
clawing at the plastic
bubble. Helen kicked
against the door but it
didn't even flinch.

Zak felt for his pager.
If he could just press
the panic key . . .
but the pager
didn't
respond.

'It's dead,' he stammered. 'It won't work in here.'

'The phone!' Helen shouted. 'Maybe the phone still works!'

She snatched it up, punched in the emergency number and waited. The rat was now running along the outside of the bubble, looking for some other way in. Zak twisted round to keep track of it, terrified by the sight of it but more afraid to look away. A woman with a calm voice came on the line and asked what service they wanted.

'We're by the Avenue,' Helen blurted out. 'Near Gordon Way . . .'

'Yes, I've traced your call. What seems to be the trouble?'

'There's a rat . . . it's trying to get at us . . .'

'There are no rats in that sector . . .'

'But we can see it!'

'One rat can't do much harm,' said the voice smoothly. 'It'll probably just run off.'

'It won't run off!' Helen snapped. 'It's . . . I don't know, it's kind of *mad*.'

'All right, caller. Stay where you are and I'll send someone round.'

'Stay where we are? We can't go anywhere!'

'Five minutes, caller. Someone will be with you in five minutes.'

Helen dropped the phone and took another lunge with her foot. There was a snapping sound and a thin splinter ran across the plastic.

'Don't!' screamed Zak. 'It'll get in!'

Helen took a deep breath.

'Open the door,' she said.

'There might be more out there!'

'Open the door, Zak! We've got to run for it!'

Helen reached for the door. Then stopped, staring at something over his shoulder. Zak turned and saw a thick-set man in a grey uniform striding steadily up the alley towards them. He had cropped hair and a face like a clenched fist, and he wore heavy boots which clicked on the road. The rat screwed its eyes shut. For a second it was quite still, then it flinched and ran back into the gloom of the alley. When the man opened the door to let them out, there was a smile on his bunched face.

'You were quick,' said Helen.

'I wasn't quick,' he drawled. 'I've been here all along.'

'All along? What do you mean?'

'Sitting over there,' he said, waving an arm in the direction of the white van. 'I heard shouting and came to see what was up.'

'But didn't they send for you?' Helen asked

him. 'Didn't you see what happened? There was a rat . . .'

'Couldn't have been,' the man said. 'You don't get rats in this sector.'

Zak looked up at his bullet head and his unfamiliar uniform and wondered who he was. Not part of the fire services or the police: they didn't wear grey. He had a black belt diagonally across his chest with some kind of case strapped to it. Zak thought it was a gun at first, but it was the wrong shape – just a narrow box.

'You must've seen the rat,' he muttered. 'It ran right by you.'

But the man just smiled and shook his head.

2

To City Hall

When they got to school, Helen and Zak had to report to Mr Sebastian's office to explain why they were so late. That didn't worry Helen: she said he was bound to understand when he heard about the rat. Mr Sebastian was thin – thin hair flat across his head, thin moustache and a narrow face. He perched on the edge of his desk as she explained.

'And there was only one rat?' he said when she'd finished.

'Yes, sir, but they aren't supposed to be in the North Sector at all . . .'

'It ran off when the man turned up, though. That sounds harmless enough.'

'I know,' Helen said. 'That was odd.'

'And the man said he didn't see it,' Zak put in quietly. 'That was even odder.'

'Well,' said Mr Sebastian, moving to the door, 'it's over, and you're both safe, so we'll say no more about it, shall we?'

Zak followed him but Helen stayed where she was.

'I've got to tell someone,' she said. 'If the rats are now up here . . .'

'If they are, Helen, the authorities know already. They'll do something about it, won't they?'

'I suppose so . . .'

'One stray rat,' said Mr Sebastian. 'I'm sure they can handle that.'

He pulled thoughtfully at his moustache.

'Tell you what,' he said. 'You need something to take your mind off all this. Maybe you could do a little job for me.'

'A job?' Helen said with sudden interest. 'What?'

'You know the Mayor has just been re-elected?'

'Yes. We saw the banners. "I'm here because I care."'

'She's holding a celebration in City Square the day after tomorrow. With fireworks and speeches from people in different branches of city life. Like schools. The Mayor wants a couple of pupils to speak from the platform. Suppose I choose you two?'

'We'd love to,' Helen said immediately, 'wouldn't we, Zak?'

Zak smiled weakly and gave an unconvincing nod. Standing in City Square and speaking to a crowd of strangers? The very idea filled him with dread.

'Splendid,' Mr Sebastian said, showing them out. 'I'll let City Hall know today.'

He watched them make their way up the corridor and Zak could hear him whistling softly through his teeth.

'We'll be up there with all those big names,' Helen said cheerfully. 'With Drina Boon, the Mayor herself! Representing the school. Representing all the schools in Grace, in fact.'

'Great,' he said faintly.

'What's the matter with you, Zak? You look kind of sick.'

'I can't talk to all those people, Helen, you know I can't. I even hate standing up in front of the class.'

'Oh, rubbish. You'll be fine. It's a great honour.'

Zak plodded along in silence behind her. Everything was moving too fast. First the rat and now this . . . trial. They reached their form-room and Helen was about to barge in, when he held her arm.

'Now what?' she said.

'The rat – are we just supposed to forget

about that?'

'You heard what Mr Sebastian said. The authorities will deal with it.'

'But that man who came to rescue us . . .'

'What about him?'

'Who was he? And what was he doing there? I have this funny feeling . . .'

'You always have funny feelings, Zak. Don't worry. We've got more important things to think about now.'

She gave him an encouraging smile and pushed into the form-room.

*   *   *

The following day – Tuesday – Mr Sebastian told them he'd been in touch with City Hall and the Mayor had asked to see them.

'Drina Boon is a busy woman,' he beamed, 'so you can consider yourselves very lucky.'

'Yes,' muttered Zak. 'Very.'

He didn't feel lucky, though. He felt sick.

'She probably wants to talk about what you're going to say. One-thirty this afternoon, all right? I'm sure you won't let the school down.'

'We'll do our best,' said Helen.

So just after lunch they picked up a free-cab outside the school gates and told it to make for City Hall. Then they sat back and watched streets and office blocks sweep silently by.

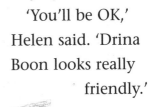

'You'll be OK,' Helen said. 'Drina Boon looks really friendly.'

'I know. I just feel a bit jittery, that's all.'

'Jittery? Why?'

He shook his head and said he didn't know. It was just a feeling. He couldn't explain the muddle of thoughts swimming around in his head. He was anxious about meeting the Mayor, yes, and having to speak in City Square, but there was something else, something more worrying. He tried to tell himself it was just his awkward imagination again, but he couldn't shake the thoughts from his mind. All last night he'd been tossed by nightmare visions of yellow fangs and clawing feet, mixed up with the hard face of the man in the grey uniform.

At City Hall they were shown up to a plush reception area outside the Mayor's office. They sat there waiting, surrounded by palms and staring at a set of double doors. Above the doors were those words again: 'I'M HERE BECAUSE I CARE.'

'Maybe she's busy,' Zak whispered. 'She should've seen us ten minutes ago.'

'Don't look so scared,' said Helen. 'She won't forget us.'

The remark stung him. She made it sound as if he was scared of everything, and he wasn't. Just then the doors flung open and a tall man in a shiny suit came out. He had silvery hair, cropped short, and he swept the room ahead of him with sharp eyes. He was followed by the Mayor. She wore a wide-collared red jacket, very business-like, and her blonde hair was scraped back in a tight knot. The face was the same one they'd seen on the banner, but without the smile. When Helen jumped up and walked over to her, the tall man blocked her way.

'It's fine, Rich,' said the Mayor. 'This must be Zak and Helen from Grace High. You'll be helping with the celebrations, isn't that right?'

They nodded.

'Well, it's a busy morning,' the Mayor continued. 'We'll talk in the car, OK?'

Moments later they were easing back on soft seats as the Mayor's car, with its sleek metal-blue lines and its darkened windows, skimmed along the city streets. Rich, the crop-haired man, sat in silence next to the driver.

'I have to open a health centre in fifteen minutes,' said Drina Boon, 'so we'd better get started. I'd like you to tell people about what we've done for the city. Not long ago we had litter and crime and foul air. People couldn't look forward to a healthy old age like they can now. We've made great advances since then. You know why? Because the Mayor cares. I care for my people.'

She went on to list all the things which

showed how much she cared. Zak tried to ask a question, but when he opened his mouth she stopped him with a lift of her hand, and talked on.

'And with the help of Mr Sebastian, our schools are the finest in the land. So, you see, there are plenty of good things for you to talk about.'

She stopped and smiled at them and Zak managed to get his question out.

'What about the bad things?'

'What bad things, Zak?'

'We saw one of the rats yesterday.'

He could feel his heart knocking against his ribs as he waited for her to speak. Her face clouded and she pursed her lips. Rich half turned from the front seat and raised his eyebrows, but she gave a tiny shake of her head.

'Why don't you tell me what happened?' she said.

Then Helen took over, describing their encounter with the rat. Drina Boon sat back listening, sometimes nodding, but with no expression on her face. Zak couldn't tell if she believed what she was hearing.

'This was by Gordon Way, was it?' she said after a long silence.

'Yes. In an alley.'

'Hmm. That's worrying. They seem to be on the increase.'

'Mr Sebastian said you were dealing with them,' Zak said.

'We are, Zak, yes,' she said quietly. 'There

have been . . . problems in the South Sector. People have been attacked. The rats down there work in packs. But I am doing something about it,' she added. 'You need someone strong to deal with this, and it's fair to say that that someone is me.'

'What are you doing?' asked Helen.

'I've formed a special team. The man who rescued you yesterday was probably part of my Rat Squad.'

'He said he didn't even see the rat,' Zak put in.

'Perhaps he was just trying to reassure you. And, after all, it ran off, didn't it?'

'Yes, as soon as he appeared . . .'

'Well, then. These rats are very large and fierce and we don't know where they've come from, but we're getting them under control. You saw that for yourselves.'

The smile returned and she leaned forward to tap the driver on his shoulder.

'Just here, Max,' she said.

The car pulled in beside a small crowd

which started cheering and waving little flags as soon as the Mayor and Rich got out. Before she left them, Drina Boon leaned into the car again to say goodbye.

'Listen,' she said, shaking them by the hand in turn, 'why don't you write out what you're going to say at the celebration and let me see a copy? If you do it on a school computer you can send it direct.'

'We will,' said Helen.

'Good. Max will drive you back now.'

Max twisted round in his seat, grinned and touched the peak of his cap.

'Tell you what, ma'am,' he offered. 'I could take them to City Hall. Show them around the new van.'

'That won't be necessary, Max! Leave the rats to those who know what they're doing. Now, I want you back here in thirty minutes to pick us up. Understand?'

For a moment Zak glimpsed something different in the Mayor's face – a kind of chill, with no trace of the kindness which smiled down from the banners. She walked off, waving cheerfully at the crowd.

No, he thought. I'm imagining things again.

*   *   *

Max was solidly built and beneath his peaked cap his eyes were creased with laugh lines. He guided the car into the stream of traffic, one hand on the wheel, one arm across the passenger seat so he could chat over his shoulder.

'She's a smart lady,' he said proudly. 'If there's a problem with rats, she'll sort it out. She sorts everything out. That's why she's mayor . . .'

'Because she cares,' Helen finished for him.

'Exactly. And that's why everyone just voted her back in. I hear you'll be talking at the fireworks display. Quite an honour, that.'

'What's this new van you mentioned, Max?' Helen asked.

'Big white van for the Rat Squad,' he said. 'They've only been using it a couple of months.'

'We saw a van yesterday,' Zak said. 'It didn't say Rat Squad on it, though.'

'No. It's not marked up yet. What's the matter with this traffic?'

They were surrounded by free-cabs and delivery vehicles, hovering and stopping, hovering and stopping.

'You could turn off the Avenue,' Helen suggested. 'There's a street that cuts through to Gordon Way.'

'I don't know,' said Zak. 'I'm not sure I want to go there again.'

'I do. I want to take another look, from the safety of a car.'

'I'm not supposed to go that way,' Max said, 'but I guess they won't notice.'

He shrugged and turned off the Avenue. For a while they began to make smooth progress again, but then the car gave a sigh, sank gently on to the road and stopped. Max frowned.

'That's a funny thing,' he said. 'It's like they've disabled it from headquarters.'

'Can they do that?' Helen asked.

'Oh, yes. City Hall can cut off the power. But they usually warn me if they're going to do that. I better take a look.'

The door opened with a hiss and Max swung his legs out.

'Aren't you scared of the rats?' Zak said quickly.

'You bet. I hate the things. But I reckon it's safe enough now.'

Helen reminded him they'd seen one here yesterday.

'Only one, though. And it ran away, didn't it?' he said. 'Anyway, she said there's nothing to worry about in this sector. I'm going to take a peep at the power supply. There should be a little green light down below somewhere.'

Zak watched Max amble up the street and crouch down to peer under the car.

He watched and waited, squeezing his fists together and trying desperately not to think about what might be scuttling in shadows.

Hurry, he thought. *Please hurry*.

But Max was taking his time.

He frowned with concentration, his eyes fixed on the bottom of the car, then, at last, he grinned and gave them a thumbs-up sign.

'We're back in business,' he called. 'Don't know what it was, but the green light just came back on.'

Zak let out a long sigh of relief and sank back in his seat. Then, as he glanced at Max walking slowly back, he saw the rats streak out of the alley behind him.

3

Too many questions

There was a pack of them, huge and greasy brown, their backs arched as they hulked along. Zak's stomach knotted with fear and he couldn't make his mouth work. He heard Helen hammering on the window with the flat of her hand.

'Max!' she shouted. 'Look out!'

Max jerked his head round and for a second he froze. Then he made a frantic dive for the door. Tumbling in awkwardly, he pummelled the dashboard – once, twice – and the door began to slide shut.

The leading rat lodged itself in the gap and the door stuck. Its head twisted from side to side, and Max struck at it with his heel.

He knocked it back, but the door clunked shut on his ankle. He hit the dashboard again and when the door opened the rat was hanging from his leg. He kicked hard and sent it spinning across the sidewalk. Then the car lifted and swung away.

'Now look!' Max shouted fiercely. 'There's blood on the seats and I've got to pick her up soon.'

His face was contorted with fear and anger, and he glowered at them as if they were somehow to blame.

'What's going on here?' he said. 'Why did we stop like that?'

The last five minutes of the journey passed in silence. Max took them to the school gates and waited for them to get out, staring straight ahead with a fixed expression. They thanked him for the lift but he still wouldn't look at them.

'She said we'd be safe up here,' he mumbled to himself. 'She promised.'

*   *   *

Zak could hardly concentrate during the rest of the afternoon. He heard the teachers' voices, but they seemed distant, as if they were coming from another room. Whenever he closed his eyes, he saw the rats. In the dark of his mind they were loping along in hunting formation, closing in and looming up at him.

At the end of school, he went to join Helen in the computer room so they could work on their speech. He wasn't looking forward to it. Helen was alone, staring at one of the screens and unusually quiet. He sat down next to her and saw that she'd already made a start.

It's a great honour, she'd written, and then no more.

'Zak,' she said, without turning from the screen, 'why do you think the Mayor's car broke down?'

'No idea.'

'I've been wondering about that. And why the van has no markings on it, and what that man was doing by the phone bubble in the first place.'

She frowned and swivelled round to face him.

'There's something wrong somewhere, isn't there, Zak?' she said. 'I keep thinking of these questions and they won't go away. What are we going to do about it?'

He wanted to tell her to do nothing, leave it to someone else, but he knew he couldn't say that. Helen would keep asking, trying to find answers on her own, and if that led her into trouble . . . well, he'd never forgive himself.

'We could start by making a list,' he answered steadily. 'A list of all the questions that don't have answers.'

'Thanks,' Helen said with a quick smile. 'I didn't fancy facing this by myself.'

Then she turned to the computer and deleted the start of her speech. For the next twenty minutes they took turns at the keyboard, adding questions as they thought of them. When they sat back and stared at the screen, they found that most of them centred on Drina Boon.

'It's all down to her,' Helen said. 'You know, I don't think she's the caring person she pretends to be.'

'No,' he said. 'She gave Max a bad time when he mentioned the van.'

'Trying to shut him up, in case we got too interested in the Rat Squad.'

A series of urgent clicks from the computer interrupted her and they saw their words flicker and fade, as if they were melting, and the page replaced by a blue screen. Helen grabbed the mouse and clicked on the short-term memory programme. Dates flicked up, day by day, until it reached Monday. Then nothing. They sat blankly in front of the blank screen.

'Stupid, useless gadget!' Helen shouted. 'Don't you know today's Tuesday!'

'Shouting won't get us anywhere.'

'I know, Zak, but what a time for it to go down!'

'There's nothing wrong with the computer. It's just that file. I think it's being tampered with. From outside.'

Helen swung her chair round and stared at him.

'Drina Boon,' she said slowly. 'It has to be.'

The whole thing suddenly seemed too big for them to handle on their own. For the next ten minutes they talked it over in whispers, as if the walls might hear them. Helen said they ought to tell Mr Sebastian so they sent a message to his pager asking if he was still in school. They didn't say more than that – there was no telling who might be tuning in. A minute or two later he paged back. *Come to my office straight away.*

The office was empty when they got there. Zak sat down to wait but Helen paced up and down between a large window overlooking the city and the neat desk.

'Do you think he'll believe us?' Zak said.

'He has to, Zak; we need his help.'

A slow minute went by and still he didn't turn up. Helen noticed a package on his desk. It had the City Hall stamp on it.

'What's he getting from City Hall?' she

asked.

'Could be anything,' said Zak. 'They send out all sorts of stuff to schools.'

Helen picked it up and found it was open at one end. She eased out a narrow black box . . .

'Don't!' hissed Zak. 'He might come in.'

'It's from the Mayor's office. Do you reckon she's trying to get to him too?'

It was an unusual box. Zak knew he'd seen something like it before, but couldn't think where.

'It looks like some kind of vidi-cassette,' he said.

Then they heard the door click and Helen dropped the package back on the desk. Mr Sebastian came in looking hurried and anxious.

'Helen, Zak,' he said, 'what is all this?'

They started to tell him about the computer file breaking up, but he was shaking his head before they'd finished.

'You think the Mayor is involved in this?'

he said.

'She must be,' said Helen.

'Computers crash from time to time. It doesn't mean someone's out to get you. Especially someone like Drina Boon.'

'But she's not telling the whole truth about the rats. I know she isn't . . .'

'Of course she is, Helen. She told you about the Rat Squad and the van, didn't she? Anyway, everyone trusts her. She wants these rats sorted out as much as you do, if not more.'

'It just seems strange,' Helen said. 'As soon as we type, the screen breaks up, like someone's reading over our shoulder.'

He shrugged and swivelled round to a small screen on the corner of his desk.

'Come and look at this,' he said and began to dart the cursor round the screen. 'You think someone's interfering from outside? Well, it's easy enough to check. I just call up all the outside links made with our computers today.'

He narrowed his eyes as he worked, pulling his lips back from his teeth and whistling softly.

'Ah,' he said. 'Here we are: outside communications. Only three for today. Two from a supplier of sports equipment and one from the City Library. No one's linked with your computer since last Thursday.'

'But she has been in touch with the school today,' Helen said quickly.

'Has she? How do you know that?'

'The package on your desk . . .'

He looked sharply at the package and then back at Helen.

'Yes,' he said. 'About the celebrations tomorrow. She wants a bit more information. How did you know the package was from her?'

'I . . . I just noticed it.'

'Listen to me, Helen,' he said, folding his arms and looking at her closely. 'You've had a bad experience with these rats. It's upset you. Then you try to write your speech and the computer crashes. But that's bad luck. You can't go around accusing important people of trying to stop you. Why not go back and try again? If the computer still doesn't work you can come here and use this one. OK?'

Helen flashed a look at Zak. It was a look he'd seen before and he knew what it meant. She was angry. They'd come to Mr Sebastian for help and he was treating them like little kids. Zak stood up.

'You're right, sir,' he said with a sigh. 'We've got no proof, have we?'

Out of the corner of his eye he saw Helen's
jaw drop, but he took no notice and went on.
'We should really get on with our speeches.
There isn't much time.'

'Exactly,' said Mr Sebastian. 'And try to
forget about the rats. The best person to deal
with them is Drina Boon. Am I right?'

'Yes,' said Zak, smiling politely. 'Leave it to the Mayor. She'll sort it out.'

'Of course she will, Zak, of course she will.'

Still smiling his polite smile, Zak backed out of the door. Helen followed him, speechless and fuming.

4

Don't push your luck

Zak walked quickly down the deserted
corridor.

'Why?' Helen said, striding angrily after
him. 'Why did you back off like that? We
were supposed to convince him, Zak, and he
didn't believe a word we said.'

'Maybe,' he said.

'Now he thinks we're just wasting his time
with spooky stories . . .'

'I hope that's what he thinks.'

She stopped walking and clapped a hand
to her head in disbelief.

'You hope?' she cried. 'What's the matter
with you?'

Zak stopped walking, too. He looked up
and down the corridor and lowered his voice.

'He was lying, Helen.'

'What?'

'I don't think we can trust him.'

He glanced up at the security camera winking in the ceiling and pressed his lips together. He wouldn't say another word until they were safely outside the school gates. They sat on a bench by the beech hedge to wait for a free-cab. The sun was low in a clear blue sky and Grace City was spread out below them, its elegant high-blocks clean in the early evening light. Helen spread her hands in an angry gesture and looked Zak in the face.

'So what's this all about?' she snapped. 'Don't tell me. You're scared.'

'It's not that,' he said.

'Yes it is. You're a coward, Zak. You can't face it.'

He lowered his head and blushed. He knew she'd only said it because she was mad at him, but it hurt all the same.

'I've seen that box before,' he said quietly. 'I suddenly remembered.'

'What box?'

'In the package. It looked like a vidi-cassette but it wasn't, Helen. We saw one just like it yesterday.'

'Where?'

'The man from the Rat Squad had one.'

The anger drained out of Helen's face as she tried to remember.

'We were in the phone bubble,' Zak continued, 'and he was walking towards us. Grey uniform, black belt . . .'

'Yes,' she said. 'And a box fixed to his belt. What was it?'

'I don't know, but I reckon it's got something to do with the rats.'

'That doesn't make Mr Sebastian a liar, though. He didn't mention the box.'

'No, but there's something else. He said the Mayor told us about the van . . .'

'Well, she did.'

'I know, but we didn't tell him that, did we?'

'No,' she said slowly. 'We didn't say a word about the van.'

'So how did he know?'

There was only one way: Drina Boon must've told him. She must've phoned during the afternoon and told him everything they'd said. And Sebastian pretended to know nothing about it. Zak was right: he had lied to them.

'It wasn't Drina Boon who hacked into our computer,' said Zak. 'It was him. He keyed into our screen and when he saw what we were writing, he wiped us out.'

'But why?' she asked. 'It's crazy. Why

should he do that?'

'Who knows? All we can say for sure is that we can't trust him any more. We're on our own, Helen.'

Only yesterday Grace City had seemed clean and fresh and they could trust everything they saw. Now all that had changed. There were rats lurking in alley-ways, and the people they went to for help turned out to be liars. They sat on the bench and looked at the skyline of slender, tall buildings. Zak usually found that a beautiful sight, but now it looked lonely and frightening.

'I'm sorry,' Helen mumbled.

'What for?'

'What I said, calling you a coward . . .'

'That's all right. Forget about it.'

'We can't forget about the rats, though, can we?' she added. 'We have to do something about them.'

'Yes, but what? We can't trust Sebastian and we can't trust the Mayor . . .'

'There's Max, I suppose.'

'I don't think he'll want to see us again,' said Zak, shaking his head. 'Not after the rats attacked him.'

'But he can't really blame us for that. And he did know something about the van. We could try him, Zak.'

A free-cab drew up and they got in. It purred, waiting for instructions.

'All right,' said Zak. 'Let's see if we can find Max.'

He knew what that meant. Let's not run away and hide. Let's risk more trouble. They paged a couple of messages home to let them know they'd be late. Then they told the cab to go to City Hall.

By the time they got there, the Avenue was bright with the blue and gold of street lamps. City Hall itself, towering up in the dusk, was a pattern of dark and light squares where some offices had closed down and some were still working. They pushed through revolving glass doors and crossed a vast, shiny floor to

the reception desk. A young woman in a red
tunic looked up from a screen and frowned.
She was used to dealing with important
people – they could see that in her face – and

they didn't look important enough to bother with.

'Yes?' she said suspiciously.

'We want to see Max,' Helen said.

'Who?'

'Max, the Mayor's driver. He gave us a lift.'

She raised her eyebrows as if she doubted the truth of that, then glanced down at a screen on the desk.

'Ah yes. I have him here on screen. Why did you want to see him?'

'He was attacked . . . I mean, he had an accident . . .'

'The rats,' she cut in. 'That's been dealt with. There's really no problem.'

'I'm sure there isn't,' Zak said. 'I'm sure it's all been sorted out. We just thought we'd see if he was all right.'

'He is. I have a message here that says he is.'

'Well, could we see him anyway?' Helen asked.

'I doubt it. Wait there and I'll find out.'

They watched her fingers jiggle over a keyboard. Something flashed on the screen, and she raised her eyebrows again.

'Oh,' she said with some astonishment. 'He says he'll be right down.'

Helen smiled to see her slightly shocked expression. The Mayor's driver, coming down to see a couple of kids? She was still smiling a moment later when the lift doors opened and someone came striding towards them.

But her smile faded when she saw a tall figure with silvery hair. Rich. Coming straight towards them.

'You wanted Max?' he said.

'We only wondered if he was all right,' said Zak.

'Why shouldn't he be?'

'We were with him when the rats went for him,' Helen said.

'He's fine. It was nothing.'

Helen was going to point out that they'd seen one of the rats hanging from Max's leg, but Rich cut her off.

'Listen,' he said, shifting sharp blue eyes from one to the other. 'Don't push your luck. Drina's taking care of the rats. That's all you need to know. So keep your noses out of things that don't concern you.'

He steered them through the doors and out into the night. As they walked away they could still feel those eyes on their backs. The threat was clear enough – stop asking questions or you'll get into trouble – but that only created more questions. What was so secret about the Rat Squad? And what would he do if they kept asking?

'Now what?' Helen said.

'I don't know. No one's going to listen to a couple of kids.'

'Maybe other kids would, though. Suppose we tell them at school what we've seen?'

'Spread the word, you mean?' said Zak. 'It's worth a try. And if we put it on paper they can pass it round.'

'Yes, make notes. But not on a computer. They'll know what we're doing.'

'No. The old-fashioned way. Writing.'

They were a block away from City Hall by this time, looking round for a free-cab to take them home. Zak thought he heard one hum up behind them, but when he turned round there was nothing there. Only a man hurrying along the sidewalk, huddled against the chill. It was a familiar figure, and he was limping slightly.

'Max?' he said. 'Is that you?'

The man looked up briefly, caught his eye and immediately set off in the opposite direction. It was Max all right. They scooted after him and soon overtook him. He was in

no mood to talk, though.

'What are you doing here?' he snapped.

'We wanted to know how you are,' Zak said.

'I'm OK.'

'And to ask about the rats.'

'I got nothing to say. Just leave it alone, will you?'

'But there are things that don't add up . . .'

'I don't do adding up. I'm a driver. You've caused enough trouble already. Why don't you go home and forget about it? You'll be sorry otherwise.'

And with that he beetled off and left them standing.

'First Rich and now him,' Helen said as they watched him go.

'That was different, though,' said Zak. 'He was scared.'

'That's no use to us, then. This is no time to be afraid, Zak. Let's get back and start on those notes.'

Imagined fears, Zak thought, or real ones?

Whatever they were, they'd have to be faced sooner or later.

*   *   *

The first person they met in the school yard next morning was Eddie. They caught him as he was about to go up the steps to the main doors. He grinned when he saw them. Eddie grinned a lot. Helen took him aside and handed him a small square of paper.

'What's this?' he said doubtfully.

'You know about the Rat Squad, Eddie?'

'No.'

'Then read it and you'll see.'

'Some kind of joke?'

'No joke. Nothing like a joke. Just read it, will you? And then pass it on to someone else. We've only got a few copies.'

He shrugged and put it in his bag without looking at it. Then he carried on up the steps.

'And don't let the teachers see it,' she called after him. 'Kids only, OK?'

'He'll forget,' said Zak. 'He's got a memory like a sieve.'

The first bell sounded and they pushed through the doors after Eddie. The lower corridor was crowded with people queuing to pass through the registration gates. As they joined the queue, Zak caught sight of Sebastian beyond the gates, and his heart turned cold. He nudged Helen. She saw Sebastian immediately and nodded back.

'Looking for us, d'you reckon?' she whispered.

'Bound to be. He's got to tell us about the arrangements for tonight.'

They shuffled through the gates and Sebastian headed purposefully over to them. He looked friendly enough but they didn't believe in looks any more.

'Zak, Helen,' he said. 'We need to have a little chat. About tonight.'

They followed him out of the throng, and into the quiet of the corridor which led to his office. When they reached his door he pushed it open. They didn't move.

'We haven't exactly written anything yet,' Helen said.

'Nothing at all, Helen?' he said, his thin face darkening. 'Are you sure?'

He gestured at the door. They stepped
inside and saw Rich propped against the desk
with his hands in his pockets.

'You know Mr Rich, I think,' said

Sebastian. 'He's got some questions for you.'

Rich put his head back and stared at them for an agonisingly long moment.

'Oh, dear,' he said eventually, 'you look nervous. Can this be right, Sebastian? Are these the pupils you've chosen to make the speeches tonight?'

'They were,' said Sebastian, 'but I think I'm going to have to change my mind.'

'That's OK,' Helen said quickly. 'We won't mind.'

'It's not as simple as that, I'm afraid. You've got some questions to answer first. Why don't you hand me your bag, Helen?'

Helen remained quite still and stared back at him. Sebastian shook his head, laughing slightly to himself, then snatched the bag from her shoulder. He took it to the desk and up-ended it. A book and some tapes spilled out. He pushed them around with his fingers, searching.

'Why don't you look inside that book?' said Rich.

Sebastian picked the book up and fanned through the pages. Several notes fluttered out. Rich took a hand from his pocket and held it out.

'I'll take them. We don't want the wrong people getting hold of them, do we?'

'How did you know?' asked Helen faintly.

'It's my business to know. I warned you yesterday, remember. Did you think I'd leave it at that? No, I had you followed. Last night and this morning. I guessed you weren't the sort to take notice of warnings.'

He turned his gaze on Zak.

'You are, of course – I knew you'd cause no bother – but you got yourself into bad company, so you'll have to pay for it, too.'

'What do you mean, pay for it?' asked Helen.

'You'll see. When we get to City Hall.'

They were led out, down corridors and across walkways, and Sebastian smiled at everyone they passed – smiled and nodded, so friendly and reasonable. When they got to

the main doors, they almost ran into Eddie
coming out of a classroom. Zak caught sight
of his puzzled face for a second, and
wondered if they'd ever see him again.

5

Into the dark

The car pulled out of the school gates and
they swept down the hill towards the city.
Zak briefly met Rich's cold eyes in the driving
mirror.

'Getting nervous?' he said staring straight at him. 'You should choose your friends more carefully.'

'You can't do this,' said Helen. 'We haven't done anything.'

'That's what you think. You've stirred up a whole lot of trouble by sticking your nose where it doesn't belong.'

'Just by asking questions?'

He grinned at the driving mirror and didn't answer. When they reached City Hall he drove round to the back, easing the car down a long concrete slope to a set of metal doors which lifted automatically as they approached. He told them to get out and they found themselves in the gloom of an underground car park, empty apart from a large white van. There was a hiss, very loud in that closed space, and the van door opened. Drina Boon stepped out.

'It's cold down here,' she complained. 'I had to wait in the van.'

Without even glancing at Helen and Zak,

she marched off towards a bulky door in the
back wall, the click of her shoes echoing
through the shadows of the car park. The
door slid open to reveal a lift. Rich gave Zak a
push between the shoulders. They stumbled

in behind the Mayor, the doors sealed smoothly, and they felt the lift move, pinging off floors as it went. Zak thought they were already in the basement, but his stomach told him that they were going down. Drina Boon caught the look on his face and smiled.

'Yes,' she said, 'we're going to the deepest part of City Hall. The secret part.'

'Why?' asked Helen defiantly.

'Well, my dear, you've asked so many questions I thought you ought to have some answers.'

When the lift stopped the sense of movement remained in Zak's stomach. It wasn't just the movement, though: it was the familiar cold feeling of fear. They walked out into a narrow corridor, weakly lit with ceiling-glow. There were no other doors down there, just a single corridor leading into the distance. They walked in silence until they reached the end and Rich clicked a key-tab at the wall. It lifted, like a portcullis, and they saw a room with a low ceiling and bright

white walls. Rich pushed them inside and
they were sealed in. Zak looked round
nervously. Three lines of long tables. On
them rows of plastic domes. There was a kind
of jumpy activity in some of them. Things
twisting round. Scratching to get out. Helen
saw them too and backed instinctively away.

'Don't worry,' said the Mayor with a brittle
laugh. 'They can't get out. Until we want
them to.'

'But if you've already caught some of the
rats,' Zak said, 'why not just tell us?'

'Because we haven't caught them, Zak.
This is our breeding station.'

'Breeding station?' echoed Helen. 'But . . .'

'Of course. We breed them ourselves.'

Two figures in white overalls were moving silently from dome to dome, pausing to tap information into mini-screens or refill drip-feeds. A third was stacking crates at the far end of the room.

'Almost ready to go, Curt?' the Mayor called to him.

He looked up and Zak recognized the man who'd rescued them from the phone bubble. He shouted back cheerily and came over, rubbing his hands on a rag and grinning.

'So,' he said, 'we meet again.'

'You said you hadn't seen that rat in the alley,' Helen said accusingly, 'but you did, didn't you?'

''Course I did. I couldn't tell you that, though. Rats are a top secret business and I had to check with the boss.'

Drina Boon sauntered between the tables, drumming her fingers against the domes. The rats made futile leaps at her, crashing their jaws against the plastic.

'Curt's right,' she said. 'The Rat Squad is our little secret. That's why there are only three people in it. Two to doctor the rats, and one to . . . well, deliver them.'

'What do you mean, deliver them?' Zak said.

'To release them. Into the city.'

She laughed again and turned to face them.

'Oh dear, you do look puzzled. Let me explain. You see, thanks to me, we have no crime in Grace City, no wars, hardly any illness. People live to a happy old age. A very great old age some of them. Have you ever thought about that? It means that as years go by we have more and more people living here. They simply don't die off as they should, and they become very expensive to keep. We have to find some way to keep the numbers down.'

'With rats?' Zak said, appalled.

'Yes. We breed them specially, a super

breed, to kill and spread disease. Of course, we control them. They won't kill too many people . . .'

'You can't,' said Helen, her eyes flashing with anger. 'You've no right to do this!'

The Mayor looked quietly amused by this outburst, and shook her head.

'I have every right,' she said. 'Grace needs rats. Don't you understand? It needs them to control the population, but also to give people a common enemy. If they have a common enemy – war or plague or, in this case, rats – then they all work together; it unites them, and they don't complain about other things. That's the whole point.'

'But everyone trusts you. If they knew you were doing this . . .'

'Some people do know. People like Sebastian. But we can't let everyone know because they simply wouldn't understand that it was for their own good. And, in the end, that's what I care about.'

'Care?' Helen shouted. 'How can you when

you're killing people?'

'A few, perhaps, but the rats don't attack everybody. We've found a way of preventing that.'

'How?'

They heard Rich's rasping laugh behind them.

'I don't think that's any of your business,' she said, with a knowing look over their heads. 'You've already found out too much for your own good. We did try to warn you, you know.'

'Yes,' said Helen. 'Like when the rats attacked Max.'

'Exactly. When we saw you were determined to keep poking your nose into everything, we arranged that little breakdown to scare you off. It worked with Max but not you, unfortunately. You had to go on with your stupid questions, which is why you're here now.'

'But . . . but you can't keep us. We'll be missed,' Zak stammered.

'No you won't. And we won't keep you. You'll have an accident. Everyone will be sorry about it, but they'll understand.'

She glanced at Rich again and gave him a

brief nod. Without a word or a change in his expression, he grabbed Zak's sleeve and began to pull him backwards.

'Let go of him,' cried Helen.

'He can't do that, my dear,' Drina Boon said. 'We're sending you out on a delivery. Curt and Rich will take you – I'm afraid I've got a fireworks display to run. But I'm sure you'll find it fascinating. Plenty to tell your friends. Except, of course, that you won't be coming back.'

*   *   *

Rich took them back up in the lift and into the gloomy car park again. He opened the van doors and bundled them into sudden darkness. Zak huddled in a corner and clutched his knees to stop himself shaking.

'We're in real trouble now, aren't we, Zak?' Helen said in a broken whisper.

The fear in her voice startled him. From the start he'd been the one to brood on the dangers ahead, while Helen ploughed on, bold and forthright. Now she saw, as if for the first time, just what they were facing and she wasn't prepared for it.

'We're not finished yet,' he said, and smiled even though she couldn't see him.

'Zak, I can't see,' she said. 'I can't stand the dark. I can't stand it.'

'You'll be all right. I'm right here.'

He knew then that he had to fight down his own fear. He had to stay calm for both of them. Footsteps sounded outside and the van door hissed open a crack. Curt and Rich were standing by two piles of heavy crates.

'We've got some friends to keep an eye on you,' said Rich.

They began to load the crates into the van. Across the end of each crate was a wire mesh, and through this they could see the rats, lifeless and silent.

'We've given the little devils something to knock them out,' Curt said brightly. 'They won't wake up till we want them to.'

He slammed the doors and nightmare darkness closed in on them again. Helen caught her breath and grabbed Zak's arm. Her fingers dug into his skin as the van began to move off.

'It's all right,' he said again. 'I'm still here.'

*   *   *

When Curt opened the doors again light
flooded in. It was a dull light but after the
darkness of the van it still made Zak's eyes
sting. Helen was curled up on the floor with
her arms over her head.

'We've arrived,' Curt said, grabbing a fistful of Zak's shirt and dragging him out. 'Nice quiet area. Just right.'

They were in an unlit cul-de-sac between high windowless walls, somewhere on the other side of Grace City, Zak guessed. There was a rattle from the van and he saw the first rat begin to stir. It grabbed the wire with pink hands and its snout twitched.

'You're not going to let them loose?' Zak said to Curt.

'Don't rush me. I've got to sort these out first.'

He was holding two narrow black boxes,
like the one they'd seen on Sebastian's desk.
He handed one to Rich
and began to fix the
other to his belt.

'Don't
want any
accidents,' he
said. 'They'll go
for us if we don't put these on.'

So that was the point of the boxes. They
stopped the rats attacking, probably by
sending out some signal. That's what Drina
Boon meant when she said they could

control the rats. People like her, and Sebastian, would be perfectly safe while they had one of the boxes.

'We've only got two,' Curt chortled, dragging out a crate and dumping it on the road. 'Sorry about that.'

He was about to release the catch when Rich snapped at him.

'Not yet, you fool. Give me a hand with this box.'

For a second both men had their heads down as they fiddled with the box on Rich's belt. Zak saw his chance. He ran at Rich, pushing him hard in the chest with both fists. Rich grabbed at Curt to steady himself, pulling the other man off balance.

'Run!' Zak shouted at Helen. 'Run as fast as you can!'

But Curt was ready for them, looming with his arms spread to catch them.

'Let them go!' Rich screamed at him.

Curt stopped, puzzled, and let his arms drop.

'The rats, you fool! Let the rats go!'

As Curt lunged for the crates, Helen and Zak charged past, one on either side. Ahead, the alley opened onto a side-street. A narrow gap between high buildings. A slim chance of escape . . .

They ran for it, the twanging of catches and the frenzied squealing of rats sounding behind them. They were almost there when a car with darkened windows turned smoothly into the alley and stopped. It filled the space, blocking them in.

'No!' Zak yelled.

Helen stumbled to a halt, gasping for breath, confused and on the point of giving in. With a sigh the car door opened and a bulky figure got out. He stood, feet apart, a heavy spanner in his hands. Barring the way.

Then Zak saw who the figure was.

'Quick,' said Max. 'Get in!'

6

Fireworks

The car reversed out of the alley. Out of the
back window they saw the rats streaking after
them and the two men flailing their arms
and bellowing hopelessly. Max headed for the
heart of the City, cutting across main roads,
weaving through back-streets and side-
turnings. He talked quickly as he drove.

'She's not going to like this,' he said. 'She
doesn't even know I've got the car.'

'Why did you do it, Max?' Zak asked. 'I
thought you were angry with us.'

'I was. But I had to go back to the school
to bring Sebastian to City Hall. Creepy guy. I
didn't like the look of him.'

'You're right,' said Helen. 'He's in on all
this.'

'I'm not surprised. Anyway, while I'm
waiting for him, this kid comes up to me.
Little kid with a smiley face.'

'Eddie!'

'That's him. He asks if I'm Max so I say, "Yes, how d'you know that?" and he says he's got this note and it mentions me – the Mayor's driver.'

'He must've read it after all,' Zak said.

'He says he's worried because he's seen you go off with some guy with silvery hair. So I know it's Rich, and I know you must be in trouble. And I'm driving Sebastian to City

Hall and thinking about all this rat business, and I reckon you're right: it doesn't add up. I drop him off and I'm wondering what to do next when I see the van pull out. And it's not supposed to be going out just then, so I follow it.'

They were crossing the Avenue, when the car began to fade and sink.

'I was waiting for that,' Max said, spinning the wheel so the car slewed sideways. 'They've disabled it from headquarters.'

'Then they're on to us,' said Zak.

Max said the police would be looking for them as well, so there was nothing for it but to set off on foot.

'Just keep walking,' he said. 'It doesn't matter where. We need time to think.'

They'd hardly gone a dozen metres down the Avenue before sirens began to whine in the distance. They quickened their pace. It was dark by this time, but no one was going home. In fact, the city was full of people all heading in the same direction.

'The fireworks,' said Max. 'Good. We'll be harder to find in these crowds.'

But they'll find us in the end, Zak thought. They're bound to. They'll track us from the skies with hover patrols, and beam our pictures to every police mini-screen.

'Maybe we should just go home,' Helen said, sounding small and frightened in the middle of all those cheerful crowds.

'No. They'll be waiting for you there,' Max told her. 'Keep walking.'

More and more people came out to join the throng and they found themselves swept along like logs in a river. Ahead of them a policeman appeared, turning his head to study each passing face. Zak slowed down.

'Don't stop,' said Max. 'He'll see you for sure if you stop.'

He snatched off his driver's cap and flung it among the trampling feet. A man stooped to pick it up and another bumped into him. Insults were exchanged and, while the policeman waded in to sort it out, they slipped by unnoticed. A block away from City Square, they heard a voice, magnified by giant speakers, echo off the buildings and boom through the air above them.

'Citizens of Grace! Welcome to our great celebration!'

It was Drina Boon, and her words were greeted by waves of cheering.

'You have chosen me as your mayor again

so I'm sure you know – I'm here because I care!'

Another rumble of cheering. They were now in the Square itself, hemmed in by the delighted crowd.

'I've got some people here who want to tell you all about this great city of ours!'

Between bobbing heads they saw a platform draped in ribbons and banners, right in the middle of the Square. Drina Boon was standing by a bank of microphones, both arms raised in triumph. She turned and signalled Sebastian to come forward and begin the speeches. As he spoke, Max pushed Helen and Zak further into the crowd.

'Right in,' he said. 'We got more chance right in.'

Twenty minutes later, they'd forced themselves so far in that they were pressed up against a wall of blue cloth at the edge of the platform. Drina Boon was just about to introduce a woman in a flowery hat when she glanced down and her eyes met Zak's. For a moment she stood there stunned.

Then she shoved the woman aside and spoke urgently to Sebastian. He nodded and brought her a small panel with a single red button on it.

'And now,' she announced, 'let the fireworks begin!'

She pressed the button and almost immediately there was a booming explosion and the sky above the Square was filled with shimmering silver light. Light and sound jagged

through the darkness above
them and every face turned
upwards.

'It's no good, Max!' Helen cried.
'They've seen us!'

Max shouted back but his voice was lost in
another resounding blast. His face shone red
and green in the glow from the sky. He
shouted again, 'Split up! We'll have
more chance!'

But over the heads of the crowd,
Zak could see a helmet moving
towards them. Then another. The
police were threading through
the press of bodies, drawing
ever closer as the
fireworks crackled
and spat overhead.
He saw Sebastian
and the
Mayor,

silhouettes in a yellow cloud, directing them from the platform.

'Too late,' said Zak. 'They've got us surrounded.'

The first policeman broke through the crowd.

'I've got him!' he yelled, making a grab at Zak.

Max stepped between them and seized the policeman's arm. Sebastian, his face rigid with anger, was shouting down at them.

'Hold him! That man is a danger to the city.'

Someone screamed and the crowd surged back from the struggle. Then a second policeman fought his way into the circle and grabbed Max from behind. There was a cry of triumph from the platform and Zak twisted round to see the Mayor standing just above him, her face a grinning mixture of relief and exultation.

She can't win, he thought, she can't.

'Help me up,' he said to Helen.

She stared back at him, frightened and hesitant, but he was filled with a strange calm.

'Quickly, Helen! Now!'

He faced the platform and felt her hands pushing him. Then he swung himself up and sideways. Drina Boon shrieked above the crackle of fireworks.

'Get him off here! Get him off!'

But before anyone could grab him, Zak scrambled to his feet and darted for the microphones. A final volley of explosions echoed and faded. There was a brief silence, then

Zak's voice echoed into the night, powerful and clear.

'There's something the Mayor hasn't told us tonight. About the rats.'

The last word had a startling effect. Zak heard it repeat and ripple through the crowd, and saw a mass of faces turn to look at him. Then a great stillness descended on the Square. They were watching him, tense, waiting to hear what he had to say. Sebastian took a step towards him.

'No!' someone shouted. 'Let him speak!'

'What about the rats?' cried another.

Zak looked back and saw Drina Boon staring at him, her eyes burning with malice. But she could not move. She was powerless now and they both knew it. He spoke again. The boy who was too quiet for his own good, who hardly had a word to say for himself.

'Listen and I'll tell the truth about the rats,' he began.

About the author

When I decided to write a
story set in the future for a
change, I turned to my
notebook. Like most
writers, I keep a notebook
to record ideas when they
come to me. I jot down a
few words that I hope will
jog my memory. Sometimes
they stay in the notebook for years before I'm
ready to use them.

This time I found a note which said Rat Squad:
what would happen if rats were set loose in a
city . . . But I won't tell you what the rest of the
note said: it might give the secret of the story
away.